One Splendid Tree

Written by Marilyn Helmer

Illustrated by Dianne Eastman

Kids Can Press

*T*he houses along Belcher Street reminded Hattie of a litter of homeless puppies huddled together against the cold. Even in the bright December sunlight they looked gloomy.

"Race you home!" Junior shouted, thumping past in his oversized boots. He slid to a stop in front of Number Fifteen, scrambled up the steps and disappeared inside.

Hattie stared at the shabby building. It was big and old, the color of sun-baked dirt. How can Junior call this place home, she wondered. Home is our pretty green and white house on Maple Street with the big front porch, shade trees in the yard and all of us together. It isn't Momma working all day in a factory. It isn't Daddy gone off to fight in a country far away. And it surely isn't this tiny apartment Momma said we were lucky to find with so many people taking wartime jobs in the city.

Junior yanked the door open. "Come quick, Hattie! I've got the best thing to show you." He ducked back inside.

Hattie sprinted after Junior and caught up with him on the third floor landing. "What is it?" she gasped.

Junior pointed a mittened finger, grinning from ear to ear. "Look! Our plant's still here."

Hattie clamped her hands on her hips. "Is that what you're so excited about?" she huffed. "It isn't even ours. It's just a droopy old thing that got left behind when someone moved."

Junior's face fell. "If nobody else wants it, why can't it be ours?"

"It's too big for our tiny apartment," Hattie said. "Just leave it be."

"But I like it, Hattie," Junior said, wiggling a finger through a hole in his mitten. "It's big and green and it makes me think of Christmas."

Hattie started down the hall. Slowly Junior clumped after her.

Christmas was only two weeks away, and it seemed that Junior could think of nothing else. But this year would be different. They weren't going to have a tree. When Momma had explained about the war and Daddy being away and there being no extra money, Hattie had put on a brave face. But not Junior. "It won't be Christmas without a tree," he said over and over again.

"Quit clumping your feet," Hattie cautioned now. "Crabby Mrs. Dixon in 3C's going to yell at us again."

"These old boots of yours are too big for me," Junior said. "I wish I had new ones."

"I'm wearing too-small shoes that pinch my feet," Hattie reminded him. "We have to wear what we've got. It's more important for the soldiers to have boots and shoes for fighting in the war."

"I wish the war were over," Junior said. "I wish we could have a Christmas tree. Most of all, I wish Daddy would come home. If Daddy were here, we'd have a tree no matter what."

A lump rose in Hattie's throat. "Well Daddy's not here. And it wouldn't be right to waste money on a tree. We should buy Victory Bonds and war savings stamps to help the soldiers," she said, using Momma's words.

Junior was silent for a moment. Then he exploded with, "Hattie, we don't have to buy a tree. We can decorate the plant!"

"That ugly old thing?" Hattie stared at Junior. "It's too big. There's no room for it in our apartment."

"We can leave it right here in the hall. That way everyone can see it." Junior spun around, arms flung wide.

Hattie frowned. It would take a whole lot of magic to turn that droopy old plant into a Christmas tree.

"Please, Hattie?" Junior pleaded. Hattie glanced at her brother. His face was filled with hope.

She studied the plant, trying to imagine what it would look like dressed up in Christmas finery. Her frown faded as she began to catch Junior's excitement. Didn't Daddy always say that Christmas is a time when magical things happen? Decorating the plant was just the kind of thing he would do. It would be almost like having him home.

"Junior, let's do it!" she cried.

Junior dragged her toward their door. "Come on. We have to find our decorations."

Decorations! "Oh, Junior," said Hattie, "we don't have any decorations. They're at Grandma's with all the other stuff we didn't have room for."

Junior's face crumpled like a burst balloon.

Hattie remembered how she had felt when Momma said they wouldn't have a tree. But now, maybe they could. Suddenly she had an idea. "We'll make our own decorations!" she said, grabbing Junior in a hug.

"Like we do at school," Junior whooped. "We'll have the best Christmas tree ever!"

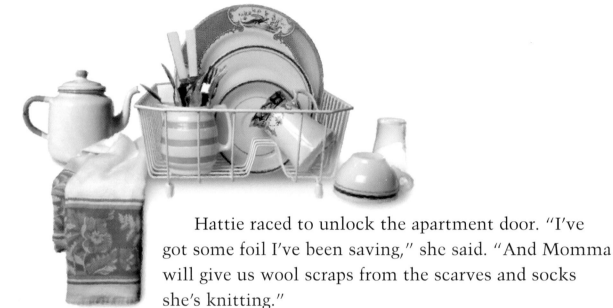

Hattie raced to unlock the apartment door. "I've got some foil I've been saving," she said. "And Momma will give us wool scraps from the scarves and socks she's knitting."

"I'm going to make paper chains." Junior dashed off to find crayons and scissors.

By the time Momma came home, the table was covered with paper and paste and snippings and clippings. When she heard their plan, she didn't even make them clear the table for dinner. They ate standing at the kitchen counter. Afterwards Hattie and Junior hurried through the dishes.

"What are you making?" Junior asked, looking over Momma's shoulder. She was winding wool around a small square of cardboard.

"Your Aunt Louise and I made snowmen like this for our tree," she said, showing him how. Junior began working on his own and Momma picked up her knitting.

Meanwhile Hattie carefully twisted her precious foil into twinkling icicles and sparkling stars. She held one up for Momma and Junior to see. It spun in her fingers, catching the light. "Like the Bethlehem star," she said.

"Momma, Hattie, look!" Junior held up his first snowman.

Momma peeked over her glasses. "That's as fine as any I've made," she said.

Magic was everywhere that evening. The radio didn't fade and crackle the way it usually did. Carols poured out as though a choir were right there in the room. Beyond the dark window, a garland of stars glittered in the cold night sky.

When she'd used up the last bits of foil, Hattie started tying her hair ribbons into bows.

Junior raced back and forth between the apartment and the hall. First he needed a dust cloth, then a watering can, then string for his snowmen. A moment later he was back, jiggling the table. "Can I hang your icicles and stars, Hattie? Please?"

Hattie wanted to hang them herself. But she knew that Daddy would have said yes, so she did too.

Junior dashed off and was back moments later. "Come see our tree now," he ordered.

As they went out into the hall, crabby Mrs. Dixon poked her head out of 3C. She looked past Hattie at the plant and then at Junior. To Hattie's relief, Mrs. Dixon didn't scold. She closed her door quietly, but not before Hattie saw her smile.

"Momma, Hattie, what do you think?" Junior bounced up and down like a jack-in-the-box.

The plant stood proudly in the middle of the hall. Hattie could have sworn it had perked up and grown taller. Junior's snowmen and paper chains dangled from the branches and Hattie's stars and icicles sparkled in the light.

"It's like a real Christmas tree," Junior said, awed.

Hattie glanced at Momma. The tired lines on her face had been erased by a smile. Momma squeezed Hattie's hand. "That is one splendid tree," she said.

On the way home from school the next day, Junior chattered till Hattie's ears hurt. "Betty Jane Lawson showed me how to cut out paper snowflakcs. I'll teach you, Hattie," he said, all important. "And Mrs. Mackie gave me some scraps of red paper. There's writing on one side but we can use the other."

"I took some tin can lids from the metal scraps I'm collecting for the Salvage Drive," said Hattie. "I'm going to decorate them with wool and trimmings."

A surprise was waiting for them when they opened the door of Number Fifteen. The plant now stood in the front lobby. "Somebody moved our tree," Hattie exclaimed.

Junior grabbed her sleeve. "Look!"

Hattie's eyes followed his finger. Near the top hung two shiny silver bells. A popcorn chain looped around the middle.

"It's magic, Hattie," Junior whispered.

"Maybe," said Hattie, hoping that it was.

The next morning they found a bright red scarf wrapped around the plant's cracked pot. And there were more decorations — snow scenes cut from cards, cotton batting Santas and wonderful straw stars.

That evening there was a knock on the door. When Momma opened it, a white-haired man greeted her, smiling broadly. "I'm Will Stevens from 2B," he said. "That's one fancy Christmas tree you're decorating in the lobby."

Junior squeezed around Momma. "Everyone's helping," he said.

"You're right about that," said Mr. Stevens. "So I thought it would be nice if we all got together on Christmas Eve. Mrs. McMurtry in 2A said she'd save her sugar rations and bake cookies. I'll make fruit punch. You will come, won't you?"

"We'd love to," Momma said. "I'll bring my special fudge."

Hattie knew they'd have to watch their rations more carefully than ever. But, oh, it would be worth it. Just thinking about cookies and fruit punch and Momma's fudge made Hattie's mouth water.

The next few days passed quickly, filled with hustle and bustle. A dazzling snowfall decorated the houses along Belcher Street in winter glory. Hattie saw Mrs. Dixon hanging a pine wreath on the front door. And whenever he met them, Will Stevens greeted Hattie and Junior with a hearty "Hello!"

Now when Junior shouted, "Race you home!" after school, Hattie was off like the wind. She arrived first, breathless and eager to see what new decorations they would find on their tree.

Finally it was Christmas Eve. Junior was so excited he couldn't stand still. Hattie danced about in her Sunday-best dress. "Hurry, Momma," she begged when they heard doors opening and voices in the hallway.

Momma held them back for a moment. "Before we go downstairs, something came from Daddy." She brought out a small package. "He wanted us to open it on Christmas Eve. You first," she said, giving it to Hattie.

Hattie's heart jumped to her mouth. She peeled away the brown paper to save. Then she handed the box to Junior. He pulled off the lid.

On a bed of tissue paper lay a delicate golden angel. Beneath it was a note. Hattie scrambled it open. *To my angels — for the best Christmas tree ever. Love, Daddy.*

"Daddy knew," Junior whooped. "He knew we'd have a Christmas tree!"

"He knew we'd make our own magic," Hattie marveled.

Hand in hand, Momma and Hattie started downstairs. Junior raced ahead.

Apartment doors stood open. Delicious smells filled the air and the buzz of happy chatter made Hattie's heart sing. Her eyes went to the tree. How beautiful it looked. If only Daddy could be here to see it, too.

Junior held up the golden angel. "Look what my Daddy sent us," he said, bouncing from foot to foot. "I want to put it right on top."

"I'll give you a hand," said Will Stevens, and he lifted Junior high onto his shoulders.

Everyone gathered around as Junior carefully placed the angel on the topmost branch. He clapped his hands in delight. "We did it!" he cheered. "We made the best Christmas tree ever!"

"We surely did," said Hattie. The words spread a smile right across her face. "Merry Christmas, Daddy," she whispered.

To my great-aunt, Irena Pogodzinski, whose beautiful straw stars decorate many a splendid tree — M.H.

To my father, Richard Griffith, who served in the Royal Canadian Air Force during World War II. His portrait appears on top of the radio in these illustrations. He was the magic in my childhood. — D.E.

Kids Can Press acknowledges the financial support of the Government of Ontario, through the Ontario Media Development Corporation's Ontario Book Initiative; the Ontario Arts Council; the Canada Council for the Arts; and the Government of Canada, through the BPIDP, for our publishing activity.

Published in Canada by
Kids Can Press Ltd.
29 Birch Avenue
Toronto, ON M4V 1E2

www.kidscanpress.com

The artwork in this book was rendered in Photoshop. The text is set in Trump Medieval.

Edited by Debbie Rogosin
Designed by Julia Naimska
Printed and bound in China
This book is smyth sewn casebound.

CM 05 0 9 8 7 6 5 4 3 2 1

Published in the U.S. by
Kids Can Press Ltd.
2250 Military Road
Tonawanda, NY 14150

Library and Archives Canada Cataloguing in Publication

Helmer, Marilyn
    One splendid tree / written by Marilyn Helmer ; illustrated by Dianne Eastman.

ISBN 1-55337-683-8

1. Christmas stories, Canadian (English)
I. Eastman, Dianne II. Title.

PS8565.E4594O54 2005   jC813'.54
C2004-907187-4

Kids Can Press is a **Corus**™ Entertainment company

MAKE YOUR OWN SNOWMAN!

You will need

• White, 4-ply worsted wool — one 50 g (1.8 oz.) ball makes several snowmen • Piece of cardboard, 11 cm x 5 cm (4 1/2 in. x 2 in.)
• Wool scraps for hand and foot ties • Beads, wool scraps or felt for eyes, nose and mouth • Ribbon or wool for scarf
• A ruler, scissors and white glue

To make body

1. Cut 4 lengths of wool 30 cm (12 in.) each for body tie pieces. Set aside.

2. Wind wool around cardboard 50 times as shown. Carefully slide wool off cardboard.

3. Thread a tie piece through the loops at one end and tie it firmly to make top of head. Smooth ends into body.

4. With another tie piece, tie 2.5 cm (1 in.) from top of head to make neck. Smooth ends into body. Set aside.

To make arms

1. Wind wool around cardboard 20 times as shown. Slide wool off cardboard.

2. With a scrap of wool, tie 0.5 cm (1/4 in.) from each end to make hands.

3. Insert arms into body through loops below neck.

4. With another tie piece, tie just below arms to make waist. Smooth ends into lower body.

5. Cut open hand loops and trim.

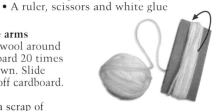

To make legs

1. Cut open all loops at bottom of snowman.

2. Divide wool in half below waist.

3. With another scrap of wool, tie 0.5 cm (1/4 in.) from each end to make feet.

4. Trim feet to match hands.

Now your snowman needs eyes, a nose and a mouth. You can give him a hat, scarf and buttons, too, or use your own ideas. Attach the last tie piece to the top of his head, and he's ready to hang on the tree!